'That bird,' said Old Smelly, 'picked a winner. Or I should say, he pecked a winner. By making a hole. Just like that hole I found the other day – at Redcar, wasn't it. Lucky Choice, that was it. You don't suppose, do you, that that bird could have . . . known?'

The sparrows all cheeped loudly, but whether in agreement or not Old Smelly could not tell. He shook his head and grinned to himself under his filthy beard.

'What rubbish!' he said to the sparrows. 'I must be going bonkers. Why, to do that, that bird would have to have, what do they call it – Extra Sensory Perception, that's it. E.S.P.!'

Eric Stanley Pigeon has an extraordinary gift – as Old Smelly, the tramp, soon discovers. For the bird can pick a winning horse by pecking out its name from a list of runners in the newspaper. Together, Old Smelly and E.S.P. seem to make an unbeatable team. But can it last?

Titles available by award-winning author
Dick King-Smith

Published by Corgi Pups
HAPPY MOUSEDAY

Published by Doubleday/Young Corgi

THE ADVENTURES OF A SNAIL
ALL BECAUSE OF JACKSON
BILLY THE BIRD
THE CATLADY
CONNIE AND ROLLO
E.S.P.
FUNNY FRANK
THE GUARD DOG
HORSE PIE
OMNIBOMBULATOR
TITUS RULES OK!

Published by Doubleday/Corgi Yearling

A MOUSE CALLED WOLF
HARRIET'S HARE
MR APE

Published by Corgi Books

THE CROWSTARVER
GODHANGER

E.S.P.

E.S.P.
A YOUNG CORGI BOOK : 0 552 55393 X

First published in Great Britain in 1986 by
Marilyn Malin Books in association with Andre Deutsch Ltd
Based on original design by Belitha Press

PRINTING HISTORY
Young Corgi edition published 1989
Reissued edition published 1998

Set in 18/24pt Garamond
by Colset Private Limited, Singapore.

Young Corgi Books are published by Random House Children's Books,
61–63 Uxbridge Road, London W5 5SA,
a division of The Random House Group Ltd,
in Australia by Random House Australia (Pty) Ltd,
20 Alfred Street, Milsons Point, Sydney, NSW 2061, Australia,
in New Zealand by Random House New Zealand Ltd,
18 Poland Road, Glenfield, Auckland 10, New Zealand
and in South Africa by Random House (Pty) Ltd,
Isle of Houghton, Corner of Boundary Road & Carse O'Gowrie,
Houghton 2198, South Africa.

Printed and bound in Great Britain by
Cox & Wyman Ltd, Reading, Berkshire.

DICK KING-SMITH

E.S.P.

Illustrated by Peter Wingham

1. Redcar

Eric Stanley Pigeon was born above a newsagent's shop. Quite high above, in fact. On the roof. He was born in a nest in a gulley between a skylight and a chimney-pot.

Because he was Mr and Mrs Pigeon's first baby, there was some discussion about what they should call him. Mr Pigeon rather fancied 'Walter', but Mrs Pigeon said 'Pooh-pooh!' to this and reeled off a selection of names of her own choice. To each of these Mr Pigeon merely remarked 'Coo!' In the end it was decided (Mrs Pigeon decided) that the child should be named Eric (after Mr Pigeon) and Stanley (after a favourite great-uncle).

When Eric Stanley Pigeon's eyes opened, the first thing upon which they focused was a sheet of newspaper. Mrs Pigeon had not bothered with much of a nest, but she had decorated the site with a few oddments picked up

from the pavement below – a cigarette packet, some milk-bottle tops, a sweet-wrapper and the piece of newspaper. Thus it was that Eric Stanley Pigeon's first experience of the printed word came in the shape of the racing page of *The Daily Echo*, informing him of the runners and riders for the meetings at Redcar and Uttoxeter, six weeks earlier.

Something about the lists of horses seemed to attract Eric

Stanley Pigeon, and he began to peck vigorously at one particular name.

'Leave that alone, Eric Stanley!' said Mrs Pigeon sharply. 'You don't know where it's been.'

There is no telling whether Eric Stanley Pigeon would have obeyed his mother, for at that moment a gust of wind came swooping across the roof-tops and caught the sheet, sending it twirling away. It floated across the street below, and over a wall

into what was locally known as 'The Park'.

The Park was an area of dirty grass and dusty trees, with a few swings and a seesaw in one corner, and a couple of benches that

had long forgotten the feel of a lick of paint. On one of these benches there sat a tramp.

For the tramp, the Park was home, and there he was a familiar figure, known to all (with good

reason) as Old Smelly. With a last tired flap, the racing page of *The Daily Echo* landed in his lap.

Newspapers were very important to Old Smelly. Sometimes the newsagent would let him have the odd unsold copy from the previous day but mostly he relied on finding discarded papers that people had read and dropped into rubbish bins. He collected them in a sack. He needed them, not primarily to read, but to cover himself at night. Others might sleep under sheets and blankets or duvets, but Old Smelly slept under a thick layer of newspapers. The only parts of them that he did read were the racing pages, for Old Smelly was a gambler. Backing horses was what had brought him to his present state, and even now, when he had no money to lose, the subject was of absorbing interest to him.

He smoothed out the page that had come from Eric Stanley's nest and ran his eye down it. There was a mark, he noticed, against the name of one of the runners in the 2.30 at Redcar, a small hole in the paper, as though someone had stuck a pin in it. Lucky Choice, the horse was called. He looked at the date on top of the page. March 5th.

Old Smelly sat in the April sunshine and was suddenly curious to know if the choice had been lucky. He reached into his old sack, and after a good deal of

searching found a copy of *The Daily Echo* for March 6th. He turned to 'Yesterday's Racing Results'.

'*Redcar. 2.30. 2 Mile Handicap Hurdle,*' he read. '*1. Lucky*

Choice. 10-1.' Nice odds, thought Old Smelly. I wish I could pick 'em like that.

2. Newmarket

Halfway through May, Eric Stanley Pigeon made his maiden flight. For some time he had been practising beating his wings up and down, and one day it was plain to his parents that he would soon be leaving home. This, they agreed privately, would be a relief, for he took a great deal of feeding. But they considered it their duty to prepare him for the wide world beyond the roof of the newsagent's shop.

'Now humans are generally all right,' said Mrs Pigeon, 'the big ones anyway – the little ones might chuck things at you – but don't trust their dogs, Eric Stanley, d'you hear me?'

'Dogs! Coo!' said Mr Pigeon.

'And, specially, watch out for cats.'

'Cats! Coo-er!' said Mr Pigeon.

'And I shouldn't go too far to start with,' said Mrs Pigeon. 'Just as far as the Park. There are no cars in there, or nasty motorbikes.'

'Vroom-vroom-vroom!' said Mr Pigeon loudly.

So when the moment came, that's where Eric Stanley Pigeon went.

In the middle of a training

session, the wind once more sneaked over the roof-tops and lifted Eric Stanley off the nest and over the edge of the roof. Flapping madly, he cleared the busy noisy street beneath, and saw below him an open grassy space. Here he landed, rather too fast, so that he tipped forward on to his beak. Recovering his balance, Eric Stanley Pigeon looked up to find himself staring at a large pair of boots, out of the toecaps of which peeped some filthy toes.

'Hullo, young feller-me-lad!' said a voice. 'Crash-landing that were, if ever I seen one. You wants to get your under-carriage down a bit smarter.'

Coo! thought Eric Stanley, this

must be a human, and a big one too. Well, Mum said they were O.K.

He ran his gaze upwards, from the battered boots to the torn trousers to the old overcoat, and finally to the face that was peering down at him, a face that was covered in a great matted bush of hair. Funny-looking things, humans, thought Eric Stanley. At that moment a piece of bread was dropped in front of him.

Old Smelly had had a particularly good morning. The greengrocer had given him a couple of bruised apples and a handful of carrots out of the box marked 'For Rabbits', the girl in the baker's shop had slipped him a whole stale loaf, and at the newsagent's they had let him have a copy of one of the previous day's unsold newspapers. He had been reading this – the racing pages – when Eric Stanley arrived, and now laid it down open on the bench beside him.

'Was that nice, young feller?' said Old Smelly. 'Have a bit more,' and he crumbled some more bread over the paper.

'Jump up here,' he said. 'I shan't hurt you.'

The noises the human was making meant nothing to Eric Stanley, but the bread had tasted good, so he did as he was bid. Like most birds, he had no sense of smell, so that getting close to the tramp did not worry him as it would have worried another human, and he gobbled up the crumbs eagerly. Then, it seemed, something on the printed page caught his attention and he began to peck again, not at the bread but at the paper itself, at one particular place. He pecked in fact until his beak made a small hole in the page. Then he flew away.

Old Smelly put the rest of the loaf back in his filthy pocket and picked up his paper again. He looked at the little hole that the young pigeon had made at the end of a line. He ran his filthy finger-nail along the line, which gave details of a horse entered in the 4.10 race at yesterday's Newmarket meeting. Jamonit was the animal's name.

Old Smelly scratched his filthy head with his filthy finger-nail, stuffed the newspaper into his other filthy pocket along with the apples and the rabbit-carrots, and made off across the Park towards the betting-shop.

The betting-shop manager was not keen on having Old Smelly in his shop – it was bad for custom – but the tramp's luck held. The manager was busy and did not see him as he slipped in and stood before the pinned-up lists of yesterday's racing results.

'*Newmarket. 4.10,*' read Old Smelly. '*1. Jamonit. 12–1.*'

Back on his bench, Old Smelly sat deep in thought. Then he gave voice to his thoughts, to an audience of sparrows.

'That bird,' said Old Smelly, 'picked a winner. Or I should say, he pecked a winner. By making a hole. Just like that hole I found the other day – at Redcar,

wasn't it. Lucky Choice, that was it. You don't suppose, do you, that that bird could have . . . known?'

The sparrows all cheeped loudly, but whether in agreement

or not Old Smelly could not tell. He shook his head and grinned to himself under his filthy beard.

'What rubbish!' he said to the sparrows. 'I must be going bonkers. Why, to do that, that bird would have to have, what do they call it – Extra Sensory Perception, that's it. E.S.P.!'

3. Newbury

Eric Stanley Pigeon flew gaily over the Park the following morning. He had now gone solo for a good many hours and had mastered the art of flight and its necessary accompaniments,

take-off and landing. He landed
now, in one of the dusty trees, and
looked down at the scene below.

The human was sitting, as
usual, on his bench. At his feet
there strutted and bobbed and
cooed a whole crowd of pigeons,
including Eric Stanley's parents.

'How in the world am I going
to be able to tell you apart from
the rest?' said Old Smelly to the
bluey-grey look-alike throng, as
yet another flew down from the
tree above to join it. As if to

answer his question this last bird flapped up on to the bench beside him.

'Eric Stanley!' called Mrs Pigeon sharply. 'Come down off there at once, d'you hear me?' But just then Old Smelly reached under the bench for his sack. At the movement all the birds on the ground flew away. The tramp studied the remaining pigeon. Then he took out an old newspaper and opened it, carefully, at the 'Today's Radio and Television' page.

Eric Stanley made no move.

Gently, slowly, Old Smelly turned the sheets until he reached the racing pages. Immediately the pigeon walked on to the paper and began to peck. Peck, peck, peck, peck he went, at the one spot, until a little hole appeared beside the name of a horse.

The tramp did not bother to look at it, or at the date of the old yellowing newspaper.

'Whatever nag that was, my

lad,' he said to the bird, 'one thing's certain. It was first past the post next day. You're my boy all right, you're the one with the Extra Sensory Perception. I think I'll call you E.S.P. Makes a nice name for you. Now then, E.S.P., what we gotta do is get hold of a copy of today's paper. Then you can peck me a horse and I'll be off to the betting-shop at full gallop. Talk about putting money on a stone-cold certainty! Only trouble is, though, I ain't even got the money for a paper. What we going to do, E.S.P.?'

'Coo,' said Eric Stanley. He was thinking about food.

Whether Old Smelly begged, borrowed or stole a copy of that day's *Daily Echo*, Eric Stanley neither knew nor cared, but when he flew back later to the bench after a few tours of the Park, he found the paper there, spread open at the proper place. More important to Eric Stanley, the tramp gave him his last bit of bread.

There were three race meetings that day. Eric Stanley showed no interest in Thirsk or Market Rasen, but walked straight to the list of runners at Newbury and began to peck at a point in the

4.30 until that little hole appeared.

'Here, shift over, E.S.P.,' said Old Smelly. 'Let's have a dekko. Nice Surprise, is it? Never heard of him but it will be, for sure. If I only had the lolly.'

Eric Stanley, having pecked his horse, was not interested in all the noises the human made, and he had strutted off down the tarmac path, investigating, as pigeons do, anything and everything on the ground. Like most places in the Park, it was thick with rubbish. Beer-can tops, spent matches, old ice-cream tubs – all were examined by young Eric Stanley in his search for something to eat; and then suddenly his eye was caught, on that bright warm morning, by a smallish round object. The sun glinted on its flat surface.

He picked it up in his beak to see if it was edible. Finding that it wasn't, he dropped it. It tinkled. Eric Stanley rather liked the noise it made, and he walked back towards the bench, picking up this new toy and dropping it again. He dropped it, eventually, at Old Smelly's smelly old feet.

There was too much hair on

the tramp's face for Eric Stanley
to see that he turned quite pale.
He bent over, stroking the pigeon
with one hand. With the other,
he picked up the pound coin.

'What a bird!' said Old Smelly
in a kind of hoarse whisper.
'What a bird you are, E.S.P.!
First you pecks the winner. Then
you pecks up the stake money.
We're in business, all thanks to
you, young feller-me-lad, and
I shan't forget what you done
for me.'

Old Smelly went into the betting-shop with the pound coin gripped tightly in his hand (for all his pockets were full of was holes). He wrote out a betting-slip, and took it to the counter.

Wrinkling his nose in distaste, the manager picked up the slip between finger and thumb, and looked suspiciously at the coin.

'Where d'you get that from?' he said sourly.

'Friend give it to me,' said Old Smelly.

A picture of E.S.P. in flight came into his mind, and he grinned behind his whiskers.

'I'm putting it on for him,'
he said. 'He felt like having a
flutter.'

4. Epsom

Old Smelly waited happily in the sunshine outside the betting-shop until the results of the 4.30 at Newbury came in. Nice Surprise had won easily.

'Your friend's lucky,' said the

manager as he handed over the winnings. 'Twenty quid and more he's won. Let's hope he gives you a bit for your trouble. You could get yourself smartened up.'

Even Eric Stanley, with his very limited knowledge of humans, could see the difference in his friend, when he flew down to the bench next morning. To begin with, he couldn't see Old Smelly's toes. Gone were the broken boots and instead he was wearing a pair of wellies. Gone were the torn trousers and the old overcoat, to be replaced by a rather shiny second-hand blue suit. Gone were quite a lot of the whiskers, for the tramp had had his beard trimmed. Into the hole in it in which his lips were now visible he was thrusting a large piece of fresh bread, followed by a large lump of Cheddar cheese.

'Hullo, E.S.P.!' said Old Smelly with his mouth full. 'Come here, my son. I got something for you,' and he tipped out, on to a crisp copy of a newly-printed *Daily Echo*, a handful of chocolate drops. 'Got 'em in the newsagent's,' he said.

'Special for you. And I've still got a fiver left. For today.'

He waited till Eric Stanley had picked up the chocolate drops, and then opened the paper.

'Now then,' he said, 'what's it to be?'

It was to be a horse called Three Loud Cheers, which that afternoon won at 8–1, and turned Old Smelly's fiver into forty pounds. And each day that week, Eric Stanley pecked the tramp a winner.

Old Smelly did not use all his winnings for each day's bet. Though he continued to sleep in the Park under his blanket of old newspapers and did not allow soap and water to touch his flesh, he did buy quite a few luxuries, mainly in the way of food, and he always gave Eric Stanley a generous share. Nevertheless, all the time his winnings were growing, and so was an idea in his mind.

Like all gamblers, he had

always dreamed of one really enormous win, a win that would set him up for the rest of his life. Now, for the first time, he had enough money to make that dream come true. E.S.P. would choose the right horse. All he had to do was to put everything that he had won on it.

As May drew to a close, Old Smelly made up his mind to act. For one thing, he knew he could not count on E.S.P.'s help for ever. The bird might get killed, by a cat or a car, or it might just fly away and never come back. And for another thing, the following Wednesday, the first one in June, was Derby Day.

The notion of having a fantastically colossal win on the Derby tickled Old Smelly's fancy.

When he bought his *Daily Echo* on Derby Day, the entire centre spread of it was taken up with the great race – a picture of the favourite, a map of the course, the tipsters' selections, and the list of runners and riders. He spread it out on the bench and waited. Before long there came a whistle of wings and a bluey-grey figure landed beside him.

To a pigeon's eye (Mrs Pigeon's for example) there was a certain obvious difference of appearance between Eric Stanley and his father. To a human eye there was absolutely none. Recently Eric Stanley had been telling his parents of the excellent grub that

his human friend was providing, like chocolate drops and other sweets, and potato crisps, and biscuits, all of which the tramp bought at the newsagent's, to share between them.

'Coo-er!' said Mr Pigeon, and he secretly determined to muscle in on his son's racket.

Now he stood on the bench and waited, impatiently, while the human made noises.

'Now then, E.S.P.,' said Old Smelly. 'You listen to me. This is the big one. It's the Derby, see, and once you've pecked me the winner I'm going to stick the whole lot on it, every penny I've got, what you've won for me, all five hundred quid of it. So get on with it, there's a clever lad, and if it's a long-priced outsider I shan't object one little bit.'

He took out a tube of Smarties and emptied a handful on to the centre spread.

Mr Pigeon had never come across Smarties before, and he found that they spurted away like tiddleywinks as he struck at them, causing him to pierce a number of holes in the paper in his efforts to nail them.

'Hurry up. Don't mess about,'

said Old Smelly, and when the
bird had flown away he looked
eagerly to see what choice it had
made. Strangely, this time there
were quite a few holes, in the

picture of the favourite, in the map of the course, and in the tipsters' selections. But there was only one that mattered to him, the one that was in the right place, in the list of runners.

There it was, right bang in the middle of a horse's name. Some Hope.

Hastily Old Smelly looked at the odds.

Some Hope. 100–1 against!

Blimey, he thought, a hundred to one outsider is going to

win the Derby today! And I'm going to put £500 on it!! And that means I'm going to win £50,000!!! All because a little bird told me.

When Eric Stanley arrived at the bench later, it was empty, except for the newspaper. Out of habit now, he walked on to it and made yet one more hole in it, with a series of firm pecks against The Real McCoy, second favourite at 3–1. Then he flew off, and before long the wind took the paper and whirled it away to join the rest of the litter in the Park.

Old Smelly did not return to his bench till late afternoon. He slumped down and buried his head in his hands, the very

picture of dejection. He did not even move when Eric Stanley landed beside him, having missed his usual treats at breakfast and lunch and trusting to better luck at tea-time.

Eric Stanley pecked hopefully at the shiny blue sleeve of the tramp's jacket. Old Smelly looked up wearily.

'You let me down,' he said sadly. 'You let me down, E.S.P. A horse called The Real McCoy won the Derby. As for the one you pecked for me – you want to know where he came in? Last. Last of all, Some Hope was. The rest was gone home to tea when he finished. I tell you straight, I shan't never trust you to peck a horse no more. Never. You and your Extra Sensory Perception. And I tell you something else, I shan't never bet no more neither. It's a mug's game. Look!' and he turned his pockets inside out.

They were empty except for a betting-slip and the Smartie

tube. Slowly, deliberately, the tramp tore the betting-slip in half and tossed the pieces over his shoulder. Then he emptied the Smartie tube into the palm of his filthy hand. There were only a couple left. He sighed. Then, gradually, a smile spread over his hairy face.

'I ain't got no money,' he said, 'but I suppose at least I've got a friend,' and he gave one of his last two Smarties to the bird.

'Coo,' said Eric Stanley.

Old Smelly stroked the shining bluey-grey feathers.

'Some Hope,' he said ruefully. 'At 100–1. And I goes and puts five hundred quid on the thing. I needs my head examined.'

'Too true,' said Eric Stanley Pigeon (or that's what it sounded like to the tramp), 'too true,' and he flew up into the clean blue sky above the dirty Park.

Old Smelly watched the pigeon climbing.

'There's one thing certain, my boy,' he shouted after him. 'All this "E.S.P." business is a load of rubbish!'

THE END

ALL BECAUSE OF JACKSON
by Dick King-Smith

'I want to sail the seas,' said Jackson.
'I want to see the world . . .'

Jackson is a very unusual rabbit - a rabbit with a dream. He spends his days watching the tall sailing-ships coming and going. He *longs* to go to sea, too. So one day – with his girlfriend, Bunny – Jackson stows away on the *Atalanta* and sails off in search of a new life . . .

A fascinating and funny tale from master storyteller Dick King-Smith.

BRONZE MEDAL WINNER, SMARTIES
PRIZE 1997

'Dick King-Smith at his best . . . it stands reading and re-reading, and each time you chuckle at something different'
INDEPENDENT

ISBN: 0552 528218

YOUNG CORGI BOOKS

THE GUARD DOG
by Dick King-Smith

"Mind your ankles, burglars!"
"He's not tall enough to reach their ankles!"
"If he did, those little teeth would only tickle them!"
"Perhaps his bark is worse than his bite!"

The little mongrel puppy in the pet shop window had a grand ambition: to be a guard dog. But the other five puppies all laughed at him. How could such a small, scruffy dog possibly expect to be bought to guard a home? He didn't even have a pedigree! And when they heard him bark, they were sure he'd never be bought. For the moment he opened his hairy little mouth, out came the most horrible, earsplitting racket you could possibly imagine! Would the poor little guard dog be doomed to a lonely life in the Dogs' Home — or worse . . .?

ISBN: 0552 527319

YOUNG CORGI BOOKS

HORSE PIE
by Dick King-Smith

Three magnificent horses – in terrible danger . . .

Captain, Ladybird and Herbert – two Shire horses and a Suffolk Punch – are not pleased when Jenny, a retired seaside donkey, arrives at the Old Horses' Home. It's supposed to be a home for *Horses*, and they don't want to share their field with a common little donkey.

Then rustlers are spotted in the area; thieves who like nothing better than to steal horses and ship them abroad – to be made into horse pie! Can Jenny and her friends save the huge heavy horses?

ISBN: 0552 527858

YOUNG CORGI BOOKS

OMNIBOMBULATOR
Dick King-Smith

"OUT OF THE WAY, TITCH!"

Omnibombulator is a very small beetle – so small that his parents give him a really long name to make him feel important.

It doesn't seem to help. Earwigs and woodlice still push poor Omnibombulator around, and snails walk across him, making him all slimy. Then, one day, Omnibombulator sets out to see the world – and discovers just how useful being really small can be. It all begins when he crawls into the toe of a huge old boot for the night, and a tramp with very smelly feet finds the boot . . .

From the master storyteller, Dick King-Smith, bestselling author of the award-winning *Harriet's Hare*, *The Guard Dog* and *Horse Pie*.

ISBN: 0552 527998